Chef Philip

Has Autism

by

Jennifer Feuerbach

Illustrated by

Dean Wroth

Author sign:

Macy, Never be afraid to follow your heart!

Jennifer J Feuerbach

JASON & NORDIC PUBLISHERS, INC.

Hollidaysburg, Pennsylvania

Library of Congress Cataloging-in-Publication Data

Feuerbach, Jennifer.
    Chef Philip has autism / by Jennifer Feuerbach ; illustrated by Dean Wroth.
       pages cm
    Summary: Although his autism presents challenges along the way, Philip learns to make lemonade and to bake and decorate a cake like a professional, which makes his family smile.
    ISBN 978-0-944727-62-1 (hardcover : alk. paper) -- ISBN 978-0-944727-61-4 (perfect binding : alk. paper)
    [1. Autism--Fiction. 2. Cooking--Fiction. 3. Family life--Fiction.] I. Wroth, Dean, illustrator. II. Title.
    PZ7.F4334Che 2014
    [E]--dc23

                            2013038076

ISBN 13 978-0-944727-61-4 Paper edition

ISBN 13 978-0-944727-62-1 Library edition

Printed in the United States of America

on acid free paper

To my family,

who's love for life inspired this book, *and*

To Fr. Malcom McDonald,

who always sees more in me than I do in myself.

"Spoon!" Philip said. He likes to help Mom make dinner. Philip has autism so he only says a few words. Yet he's very smart, and he loves to cook!

Philip didn't like carrots. One day, Mom put carrots and dressing on Philip's plate. She showed him how to dip.

Mom said "Yum!"

Mom smiled. Philip liked to see Mom smile.
He gave her more carrots.

"Yum!" she said, "now it's Philip's turn."
Philip pushed her hand away and gave her
more carrots so she would smile.

Lemonade made Philip smile. He went to get some. Oh, no! The pitcher was empty.

Philip went to Mom. "More!"

Mom wasn't looking. She left the kitchen. What could he do now?

Philip thought hard. What was in lemonade?
There was lemon juice. There was sugar. You
need a big spoon, too.

Mom came back to the kitchen. "Do you want some lemonade? I want some, too!"

She put the pitcher in the sink. Philip got his stool to watch.

Mom took out a large cup with a handle. She wrote "Lemonade" on the side. "This is a special cup for cooking," she said.

Mom let Philip help measure the sugar,
lemon juice and water. Then they stirred the
lemonade and poured it into two glasses. It tast-
ed great!

Soon Philip wanted to make lemonade by himself. Mom watched carefully. He did every-thing right!

At dinner Mom said, "Guess what? Philip made the lemonade!" Everyone smiled at Philip as they drank. Philip's lemonade made everyone feel happy.

Philip wanted to make other foods. Some
were very easy. Strawberries just needed a wash.

When Philip's class made fruit salad at school, Philip knew just what to do. He asked for the spoon and stirred like a pro.

Sometimes it wasn't easy to learn to cook. When Philip filled the bathroom sink with water, and mixed different spices together, they smelled wonderful, but it made a big mess. Dad wasn't happy. He didn't smile.

Cracking eggs was fun to practice, but it made Mom angry.

The family had to eat eggs for dinner. They didn't smile.

Some days, Dad would let Philip stand on a
chair and watch him make pancakes.

That was exciting!

Lizzy, Philip's big sister, made Mom a cake for her birthday. Philip watched very closely. He was too nervous to help. It was so beautiful.

Philip looked at books about cakes.

He watched videos on the computer about making cakes.

One day, Philip saw a box with a cake on it. He had learned how to make a cake on a video. It showed how to mix eggs, oil, and water with the stuff in the box. He knew what to do.

Philip found a bowl.

Mom and Lizzy came in. "You want to make a cake?" Mom asked. She got out the cake pan and Lizzy got the oil. Philip got the special cup for cooking. It still said "Lemonade" on the side.

"No, Philip!" Mom and Lizzy shouted. "You need a different cup."

Philip believed they were wrong. He filled the cup with water. Mom grabbed at his hand, but Philip poured the water into the cake mix.

"The cake is ruined!" Mom said. She put it in the trash. Philip cried and stamped his feet until he was worn out.

When Philip came home from school the next day, there was a cake box on the table. Mom said, "Would you like to make another cake?" Philip smiled and found the bowl again.

Mom had a new measuring cup and a new special spoon, too! Both had "Cake" written on the them. Mom helped Philip measure the oil and water. The oil made bubbles.

Mom got two eggs for Philip to crack and put in the bowl. Then he stirred and stirred and stirred. The oil and water with the eggs and mix became a smooth batter right before his eyes.

Philip couldn't touch the oven, but he could turn on the oven light to peek inside. The cake grew up to the top of the pan. When Mom took the cake out of the oven, it was perfect!

Mom and Philip went to the park to let the cake cool. When they got home, Philip frosted the cake, just like the videos. He was very careful as he spread the icing. The sprinkles were a little more fun.

That night at dinner, Philip brought out his cake. Dad smiled. "Oh, good, cake!"

"Did you make that cake?" Lizzy asked. Philip nodded.

"I only helped a little," said Mom, "It's really Philip's cake."

Mom cut the cake.

Each person had two pieces. Everyone was smiling and hugging Philip.

Lizzy gave him a kiss.

"Oh, Yuck!"

Philip had made people smile with food.

Philip is a real chef!